Between tombstones and mausoleums
A play

José Díaz

Between tombstones and mausoleums
A play

José Díaz

José Díaz
Between tombstones and mausoleums
ISBN: 9798370569661
Statutory registration

December 2022

Translated from the original work "Entre lápidas y mausoleos" written in 2020.

E mail José Díaz:
panoramalatin@hotmail.com
danilza@ptd.net
YouTube - José Díaz.Escritor
josediazescritor.blogspot.com

Printed in the USA.

"Death is a punishment for some,
for others a gift
and for many a favor"
Séneca

Content

Characters in order of appearance:

All made up as La Muerte, Catrinas or La Santa Muerte, dressed in black except Goodness who without makeup is wearing a light suit and Lust who sensually made up will be dressed in red and in high heels.

Lust
Envy
Pride
Wrath
Goodness
Sloth
Gluttony
Greed

The play takes place in a cemetery at dusk. There is moonlight and mist. Candles and candles near tombstones and mausoleums. One or another grave accompanied by objects of the deceased. Near a tombstone, there are toys andwhite, violet and yellow flowers (marigolds). The deaths are not visible to the naked eye, they are all covered with a black cloth or mesh, seated and distributed among tombstones and mausoleums. Every time they appear on the scene, they take off the fabric or the mesh that covers them. Near one of the mausoleums there is a coffin. The deaths, after being shown, will move and displace at the discretion of the director. It smells of incense.

LUST: (Hidden, from a mausoleum she makes happy and sensual sounds, she is excited masturbating with a vibrator).

ENVY: (Loudly addressing the mausoleum where Lust is). Give up that vice.

PRIDE: (making a chorus to envy). Yah! Give up that vice.

WRATH: (To Pride). Look who's talking.

GOODNESS: (Walking towards the coffin. Reflecting and talking to herself). It never stops, it never stops.

LUST: (She continues excited, the sound of the vibrator is clearly heard, which will be more audible with the arrival of the climax). Oh......

SLOTH: (stretching). Why the fuck do they have to make noise?

GLUTTONY: (Throws some banana peels that he just consumed). Let me eat in peace, without disturbance.

GREED: (Taking an inventory around her, as if the cemetery were hers. Delirious). All mine, all mine. Fantastic, all mine. (She drops some coins that she later picks up) Everything is mine, everything is mine. (Looks around the graveyard, shakes the bag with the coins.)

GLUTTONY: A good digestion is a delicate thing.

WRATH: I don't like it when they don't count on me.

PRIDE: (Sarcastically, addressing Wrath) Take a selfie.

LUST: (After climaxing and releasing her last exhalation of satisfaction). Phew. That was incredible!.

ALL THE DEATHS: (There is a pause {1, 2, 3, 4}) (In chorus as they follow an imaginary character who passes between the tombstones and mausoleums-Some point at her). There goes Nona. With lots of wool and a new spinning wheel. Using threads of life to invent death (Pause {1,2}-Reiterate
LUST: (makes a sensual sound) Ah...

GOODNESS: (Which is near the coffin and referring to Lust) Again?

SLOTH: Let me rest, let me sleep.

GOODNESS: (Opening and closing the top lid of the coffin. The one that usually covers the face of the deceased). Poor creature.

WRATH: Who is it?

GOODNESS: He must have been very poor.

ENVY: (Inquisitive) How do you know?

GOODNESS: He has no make up and is half-naked.

PRIDE: (Looking at herself in the mirror, mockingly) Huy, what a sin.

GREED: It happens to the poor. Being poor doesn't pay and it's real shitty!

ALL DEATHS: It doesn´t pay, it´s real shitty!

GOODNESS: How horrible! They can't make fun of the humble like that.

GREED: The poor will always be screwed, that's why I... (Rubs his thumb over the middle finger and the index finger, to show she has money).

GOODNESS: Your greed shows your aporophobia on your skin.

PRIDE: Only when they turn to dust (points to the graves) do they even out.

ALL DEATHS: There they are equal, there they are equal. (Pause {1, 2}). Everyone, everyone, everyone. (Pause {1, 2}) They all even out.

GLUTTONY: (burps after sipping a soda). Borp!

SLOTH: (Looks at Gluttony intently.) Let me rest in peace, undisturbed. A good nap is a delicate thing. You already ate old greedy.

GLUTTONY: (To sloth) Old as death, great as a good digestion. (Contemptuous) Lazy old lady.

SLOTH: And you (Pause {1, 2}) greedy, insatiable glutton. um!

LUST: (Who has left the mausoleum. She looks very sexy and walks on high heels that she handles very well-Everyone except Gluttony and Sloth gather and follow her. She turns suddenly and faces the deaths). And?

THE DEATHS THAT FOLLOW LUST: (After looking at her as if taking inventory) Ugh!

LUST: (Challenging) What? Does it surprise you? (Deaths scatter.)

ENVY: (To Lust). Your beauty bothers me.

GREED: I need to see

PRIDE: (To Greed:). Are you blind?

GREED: (With gestuers she calls Lust's attention and as a begger with the fist of his right hand clenched she makes gestures as if a man were masturbating). See you in full action.

LUST: (To Greed). Your greed and your stinginess deprives you of joy.

WRATH: Not money.

ENVY: Wall Street! Orgies of money that I saw pass by with pain!

SLOTH: Occupy Wall Street!

PRIDE: That already happened.
GLUTTONY: Kleptocracy remained.

ENVY: The tycoons, the thieves, the corrupt, the bankers, the hoarders, the lenders, the long sharks. The Madoffs and all those bandits with starched collars and expensive ties. I envy them.

GREED: We are not to blame for your misfortune.

ENVY: I envy even the submissive and delicate woman who never finds out anything and the voluptuous lover who does know... (Money counting gesture).

WRATH: You are made to suffer.

GOODNESS: (To Envy). You have that terminal disease that does not kill or corrupts.

ENVY: (To Goodness, showing her arms and legs, indicating that she is healthy). I don't know what you're talking about, I'm healthy.

GOODNESS: It's inside, your envy kills you.

ENVY: I feel good and calm. Surely, I must be the best.

GOODNESS: How sad!

GLUTTONY: On Wall Street, some people eat money. It doesn't taste like anything, I've tried it. They want to give it the seasoning it doesn't have. Idiots!

SLOTH: Where did you say?

GLUTTONY: Wall Street.

SLOTH: Occupy Wall Street!

PRIDE: Great people, tremendous people, good people.

SLOTH: Just thinking about counting so many bills and coins makes me tired. Oh, and those pieces of paper from the shares. How awful! What sloth!

WRATH: They have good exponents.

GOODNESS: Which ones?

ENVY: (counting them on the fingers of the hand). One, two, three, four, one hundred, one thousand. All those white-collar thieves and the decent ones too.

GOODNESS: On Wall Street?

ENVY: On both sides, there are good people and bad people.

LUST: You are talking like...

ENVY: Like who?

LUST: You know like who. Don't play dumb.

GREED: Does anyone here does not want to be rich?

GOODNESS: The problem is not wealth, it is excesses.

SLOTH: Occupy Wall Street!

(Lust who has changed her shoes passes through the

mouth of the stage, very flirtatious and seductive. She looks at Greed and signals that she will not see her).

GOODNESS: (Opens the lid of the sarcophagus, looks at the deceased, and closes the lid.) This one was never private property.

LUST: (turning to the coffin). The sluttiest of ladies. (She moves flirty and seductive to a mausoleum).

GLUTTONY: It killed monogamy.

PRIDE: Tremendous woman, they loved her very much. She was gorgeous.

ENVY: Murdered decency.

LUST: What do you know about decency?

GLUTTONY: (Looking over the deaths) Few of us know about that (Pause {1, 2}) (Points to the coffin with his lips) invented being horny..

SLOTH: She screwed up the divorse.

GREED: The widower too.

ALL DEATHS: Give him, Lord, eternal rest.

SLOTH: (reflecting) Not that one, not that one, that one, leave it to me.

GOODNESS: What are we left with?

LUST: (Who has returned to a mausoleum). It is conceptual. Well... It looks like she was beautiful, nice tits, new ass.

WRATH: (as with spite) Recessed lips.

LUST: Two bodies, like many (Pause) but not mine (She contorts).

ENVY: (To Lust). You alwayshave an opinion. (Ordering her and imitating a man masturbating with the clenched fist of his right hand) Come on, let's get to work.

LUST: (To Envy). And you're crazy to see (Pause {1, 2}) and you're not going to see.

SLOTH: (doing an analysis). Rest cannot die, nor can it be given. What is that: give him eternal rest, lord?

LUST: (To Envy) You'll never see.

(Goodness moves past Gluttony. She almost slips on a peel.)

GOODNESS: (To Gluttony). Don't throw all those peel on the floor. I almost fell.

GLUTTONY: (To Goodness). You always invade other people's territory.

GOODNESS: Here, everything belongs to everyone.

GLUTTONY: You are very healthy, you are Goodness, you do not belong in this place.

GOODNESS: Public site.

GLUTTONY: Those who dwell here: neither feel nor suffer. I don't even know why they keep them.

GOODNESS: More respect for the dead.

GLUTTONY: Why don't we make a rule?

GOODNESS: Are you talking about rules?

GLUTTONY: Could it be that there would be a time for rules?

GOODNESS: Here there is only one: dust you are and to dust you will return.

ALL THE DEATHS: Into dust you must turn. (Pause {1, 2}) Dust to dust. (Pause {1, 2}). Dust to dust. (They scan the graveyard with their gazes {1, 2}). Dust to dust.

LUST: (Very flirtatious) Dust to dust, I love the dust thing.

GLUTTONY: Over there you can hear those who bring flowers.

GREED: There is no shortage of those who steal them.

GLUTTONY: Complaining?

GREED: Until you get caught, anything goes (reflecting after a short pause) plus kleptomania is a virtue. To be clear.

GOODNESS: It's a shame.

GREED: Sinful moralists talk about sin until bang! They have caught them red-handed.

LUST: These are things that one does not understand.

GREED: (To all the deaths) I'll tell you one: there was in

a great nation, a congressman, symbol of the anti-abortion movement, who sent his lover to have an abortion. I won't tell you the country because they swarm around the world (Pause {1, 2}) but you know, (Reiterative) you know.

LUST: To tell you another: the pedophile priest Marcial Maciel was protected until the end. They punished him by sending him to live a life of prayer and penance, he died peacefully. (Exclamatory) Flower of a son of a bitch!

GLUTTONY: In good Puerto Rican, he was a bastard priest (raising his tone) and son of a great whore. (Another tone) Those who he raped kept their problems.

LUST: (Loudly) And now Ratzinger!

ALL DEATHS: Ratzinger! The Meritorious Benedict XVI.

LUST: He covered up abusers when he was Archbishop in Munich.

ALL DEATHS: Ratzinger! (Pause {1, 2, 3, 4}) The Meritorious Benedict XVI.

GOODNESS: And so the hypocrisy continues. "Do as I say, not as I do" (Pause {1, 2}) and turn off the light and good night!

LUST: The bad thing is not the hypocrisy, it seems that the bad thing was the frankness. I love sex, I say it and I practice it with adults who decide it. Do you see the difference, dear?

WRATH: Are those with the flowers still around?

SLOTH: The dead love cempasuchiles (marigolds).

WRATH: So they say.

GREED: And those who steal flowers, do they sin?

GLUTTONY: Taking what belongs to others is immoral.

ENVY: I was taught that the end justifies the means.

GLUTTONY: See? That's the fuck. The animals, which these humans (points to tombs and mausoleums) say are less than they, do not take more than is necessary.

LUST: It's true.

SLOTH: Let me rest.

GLUTTONY: I see some who come very peacefully to build their altars with many flowers and food, but I also see those who arrive late to steal what they can.

ENVY: It is a personal virtue, a way of life.

GLUTTONY: And do you think it's okay?

ENVY: And why would it be wrong? The clever make their living off the assholes.

GLUTTONY: It's not fair, it shouldn't be.

WRATH: Justice is the food you eat.

GLUTTONY: They are different things. It's my Orthorexia.

LUST: Orthorexia? The more you swallow, the more you need the rest. You swallow everything.

GOODNESS: People come in mourning to put their flowers and make their altars to praise their deceased. Some are adorable and colorful, very well executed.

SLOTH: I like to sit and watch them do. They make them on the Day of the Dead.

GLUTTONY: It suits me, they leave a lot of food that day.

PRIDE: What I like about all that is the orange decoration.

GLUTTONY: I wish they did them more often. They leave food, water and drink everywhere.

PRIDE: I love the color orange, and the smell of oranges drives me crazy.

GLUTTONY: They leave many skulls that are sweet. I love them after dinner.

SLOTH: I look and rest.

GLUTTONY: In an emergency, cempasuchiles are tasty (Reflecting) well not only in an emergency, it is worth clarifying, they are beautiful and tasty.

GREED: I prefer the business of stealing the flowers. Anyway flowers are sold after placed a couple of times. That day they give a lot and get a lot of money.

WRATH: Do you see the tomb back there? (Points) his widow must have loved him very much, she comes every week and every time she comes she cries. The gravedigger on that side said the guy was bipolar and died of a fit of sanity.

LUST: The Day of the Dead here is full. They come early with flowers, food, drinks, games, countless photos and other things.

GLUTTONY: It's serious.

LUST: You see everything, here comes a lady who brings her late husband's lover.
The two cry, get drunk and leave singing.

LAZYNESS: Very calmly, I see the whole day. It surprises me to see how the bad children cry.

GOODNESS: Those who give their souls are the mothers, the poor mothers who have lost a child, for them, there is no consolation.

LUST: They submerge themselves in that terrible pain from which they never come out, from which nothing and no one takes them out.

SLOTH: They usually arrive quietly, with their eyes gone and their faces hardened by the sun and life. They sit down to speak with their dead children, to mourn them in the midst of a suffering that only they know, they are so brave and dignified they keep it to themselves.

GLUTTONY: It's true. In this place, we see everything. That of the mothers is the sincerest act because here you see a lot of hypocrisy. Many enter with a box on their shoulders, and when they leave they do not even remember the name of the person who was in the box.

GOODNESS: (Goodness, who has returned to the coffin, opens the top lid and holds her nose as if not to smell.) It smells ugly, corrupt.

GREED: Political?

GOODNESS: Yes.

ENVY: How do you know?

GOODNESS: (Opens the lid of the coffin and takes out a piece of paper that she displays at the moment of exclaiming). WikiLeaks!

(Gluttony has continued to eat and throw away peels and waste. Sloth snores softly, Envy signals to be quiet and approaches Gluttony.)

ENVY: (To Gluttony) The WikiLeaks thing left you with the face of a poet.

GOODNESS: (Thoughtfully) I remember one.

PRIDE: No one knows more about WikiLeaks than I do.

WRATH: You are like the man who knew more about everything than everyone else.

PRIDE: What is he called?

WRATH: You know who he is. Everyone knows who he is.

ALL THE DEATHS: (Looking at the audience) Everyone knows who he is.

LUST: One who was and is not.

GLUTTONY: And the other dead?

LUST: A poet.

GOODNESS: An extraordinary poet.

ENVY: And what was his name?

GOODNESS: José Asunción Silva.

ENVY: Why do you remember him?

GOODNESS: Because of Lázaro.

ENVY: Lazaro? (Goodness moves to the center of the stage. The deaths follow her with their eyes, some stop and approach.)

GOODNESS: "Come, Lazaro!" yelled at him
by the Savior, and from the black grave
the corpse rose between the shroud,
he tried to walk, with tremulous steps,
he smelled, he felt, he looked, he felt, he screamed
and wept with joy.

Four moons later, in the shadows
of the dark twilight, in the silence
of the place and the anger, among the graves
from an old cemetery,
Lazarus was, sobbing alone
and was envious of the dead.

ENVY: José Asunción Silva?

GOODNESS: José Asunción Silva, Colombian. They say that he was in love with his sister. (We hear to Lust playing with herself).

ALL THE DEATHS: We don't like death, but it has its charms.

PRIDE: Politicians are victims of fake news.

GLUTTONY: And the pimps.

SLOTH: Of those who do not steal, but do not report it either.

GLUTTONY: Those are worse.

LUST: They are here, there and there.

GLUTTONY: They sell like gentlemen.

LUST: They're realß rats.

PRIDE: They fight for the country.

WRATH: They are misunderstood.

SLOTH: They are friends of the bandits.

GLUTTONY: The immorals denounce some trophies but not the plunder.

LUST: I said they're rats.

SLOTH: They care about private life but not public life.

LUST: I said they're rats. They attack the LGBT movement, but among them are the great promoters and enjoyers. They live in the closet, and they are joyous and fucking like anyone else. Friends and pimps of pedophiles.

GLUTTONY: Another one arrived. (Goodness walks over to the coffin, opens the lid.)

GOODNESS: This one is tight.

WRATH: How so?

GOODNESS: (With hands indicates a pair of horns).

LUST: (From a mausoleum). Bastard of profession, bastard of taste, bastard of swagger.

PRIDE: There's a lot of bastards.

LUST: Illness and pleasure that many hides.

PRIDE: That there are...there are

LUST: Tell me. By the heaps, I deal with them.

ALL THE DEATHS: (Imitating a pass typical of a bullfighter) Ole!

PRIDE: Bastards that are formed, bastards that are made and bastards that are born.

WRATH: Assholes!

Gluttony and Sloth: Bastards!

GOODNESS: (clarifying to Gluttony and Sloth) Bastard, only one is coming.

ALL THE DEATHS: Bastards! (They stop and surround Sloth)

SLOTH (Who has raised his arms stretching herself sings reggaeton rhythm - The deaths make faces, with their hands they make the symbol of the bastard and gestures as if a man were masturbating)

The bastard comes out of the closet
He enjoys thinking about it a lot.
While she reaches out
He helps himself withhis hand.
For the three of them, everything is a delight.
With champagne, weed or rum
Two timing is a problem
Not for the ones that do, it is a joy
The three put together a freak show.
The one left alone enjoys thinking about it.t
While she reaches out
He helps himself with his hand
Because two timing if you understand
it's tremendously fun!

SLOTH: (Shaking off her clothes, proud of her singing and wondering to herself) And is it true that envy kills?

ENVY: (To Sloth) Did you just say?

SLOTH: Yes sweetheart. What if envy kills?

ENVY: Of course it kills. Ask me.

GLUTTONY: So much death in vain.

GOODNESS: (To Greed) And greed does it kills?

GREED: Greed can put you in jail, (another tone) when you get caught, but it doesn't kill you.

GOODNESS: Ah, the robbery scholars.

GREED: Cunning of good and evil.

SLOTH: They never rest. Always plotting.

GREED: We are experts in ambition. Usury doctors. Owners of these and other qualities that we keep (Pause) in safes.

PRIDE: I know enough about greed. It is one of my strengths. No one knows more about greed than I do.

GOODNESS: (To Pride) Is there something you don't know about?

PRIDE: I know everything, I am the one who knows the most about everything.

GLUTTONY: Like that man?

ALL DEATHS: Which one?

GLUTTONY: (To the deaths) You know who.

PRIDE: It doesn't matter what they say. I am the one who knows the most.

GOODNESS: Be careful. You could fall and poison yourself with such petulance.

PRIDE: Petulance? You are not wrong. I am what I am: the best. I'm #1

SLOTH: Wow!

WRATH: (To Pride) It is not known who is worse, you or me.

PRIDE: No one can deny my beauty or my wisdom. That some envy her is normal.

WRATH: I do not forgive. The comments, the simple comments affect me, I hate them, I hate them. They put me into an explosive rage!

PRIDE: What fault do I have for being so beautiful and so wise? To celebrate, I invented the selfie. Nobody more beautiful than me.

WRATH: Playing with my patience is reason enough. I hate those who want to be above me, and I hate those who are below me.

PRIDE: You are in second place.

ALL DEATHS: (Clap fast {1, 2, 3, 4}) (Pause {1, 2}) then slow {1, 2. 3, 4}) (Pause {1, 2}) then slower until let the clap die {1, 2, 3, 4, 5, 6}).

GOODNESS: So much self-love cannot be.

WRATH: And there is more, much more. There is hate. Wrath and Pride, we are just as detestable.

GOODNESS: What madness!

WRATH: Hate for hate. And like us, there is much more than you think.

GOODNESS: It can't be.

WRATH: Yes, it can be.

PRIDE: Wise commentary.

WRATH: I love hate and rage. I live in a state of rage.

SLOTH: I love rest.

WRATH: (In a state of catharsis. Walking through the mouth of the stage while deaths and goodness follow him with their eyes) My blood and body boil, the bones jump out of place, the teeth lose position and the bite does not fits. My eyes pop out of their sockets and I go into a trance. I achieve my ecstasy when I reach the fury of irritation. Then I lose my reason and I am capable of anything and when I say anything it means anything (Long pause {1, 2, 3, 4}) Be careful if a politician gets angry. (Another tone) Fake news! Boom! Domination.

GLUTTONY: Me, on the other hand, with little: food and nothing else. I love when they make altars. Lots of food, good fresh fruit and above all lots of pumpkins. If it reaches me, I eat even the flowers. The fluff of flowers is wonderful.

LUST: There are other, more wonderful things.

ENVY: Don't start.

GOODNESS: (pounding on the coffin a couple of times) We have a guest of honor.

PRIDE: (Looking at her nails) Who could it be?

GOODNESS: (After opening and closing the casket) Numerous medals.

PRIDE: Any of those who call themselves queen?

GOODNESS: Cold.

LUST: Medals, jewelry and lifts?

GOODNESS: Not really lifts.

WRATH: (as if guessing) I know. Elevators.

GOODNESS: Elevators.

WRATH: A military man with grandiose airs.

GOODNESS: Hot.

WRATH: Dictator.

GOODNESS: Bring hundreds of crimes and thousands of missing.

LUST: Not all military men are like that.

GOODNESS: Of course not, but this, this was one of the most wicked.

GLUTTONY AND SLOTH: Of the wicked.

GOODNESS: I was surprised they didn't give him an honorable burial.

LUST: The president didn't allow it.

WRATH: A bit of what they call justice.

GLUTTONY AND SLOTH: Justice?

LUST: Yes, justice.

GLUTTONY AND SLOTH: You can say a lot about justice.

LUST: For example?

GLUTTONY: That there are various classes, colors and levels.

SLOTH: That is the whip of the powerful.

LUST: Of the power what? (Teacher's tone) No young ladies, the whip of the powerful is us, the one with high heels and pronounced parts. They give anything. They die for it. There they fall, there they kneel. They drool. Very serious and very manly in front of you and behind closed doors they ask for rimjobs and dildos because they love to have their asses eaten in private.

PRIDE: They surrender to me.

LUST: In front of us, you see, many of those gentlemen full of power, money and aggressiveness are one dollar dolls when they are in front of a woman who pleases them in their corrupt and dark sexuality.

PRIDE: You said it well: dollar dolls.

WRATH: He who does not have a bitch has a Demon.

GLUTTONY: A lot of posture but many are shit.

SLOTH: Total lightness. So much hypocrisy. If what happened to George Floyd, if was not filmed it and threw it on social networks, nothing would have happened.

GOODNESS: Probably. The man died gasping for air in front of thousands who were able to see the crime live and direct. "I can't breathe," he said.

SLOTH: He was handcuffed, he was defeated. They lynched him.

GOODNESS: Broadcasting the execution of a human being live is surreal.

GLUTTONY: (Relating with excitement) It was an unfortunate fact. For us, who are little or not surprised by death, that lynching filled us with fury. The man was crying out for his life. "I can't breathe" he repeated and the policemen, three, pressed and another as a tyrannical guardian did not let someone help Floyd who was dying before the eyes of the world. Americans came out by the thousands demanding justice and repeating: "I can't breathe".

ALL DEATHS: I can't breathe.

GOODNESS: In many parts of the world too.

ALL DEATHS: I can't breathe.

GLUTTONY: Abuse is the first step to death.

ALL DEATHS: I can't breathe.

GOODNESS: Racism feeds it.

ALL DEATHS: I can't breathe.

SLOTH: There is a long way to go, but the four were brought to justice and that is important.

ALL DEATHS: I can't breathe.

GLUTTONY: Let them rot in jail.

ALL DEATHS: I can't breathe.

GOODNESS: 8 minutes and 46 seconds, Officer Chauvin had his knee on Floyd's neck. Something unspeakable, unbearable.

ALL DEATHS: I can't breathe.

ENVY: So much so that some talk about Law and Order and it was the least found there.

SLOTH: Racism at its finest.

LUST: No to racism, no to discrimination.

GOODNESS: Poorly trained police officers. The basis of their preparation is dominance when it should be social integration.

LUST: The cops should constantly rotate to avoid the collusion and the crime rings.

GOODNESS: They should do other jobs besides patrolling.

LUST: Which ones?

GOODNESS: They should spend time in offices, educating communities, in schools, working with firefighters, in ambulances, in parks, on youth projects. Participating in social development and leaving domination aside.

GLUTTONY: You are very innocent. After the demonstrations, everything is forgotten. A few days later in Buffalo, a 75-year-old protester who was protesting alone and in peace was flattened by the police who came to dominate.

GOODNESS: Right?

GLUTTONY: They pushed him, he fell on his back to the floor, hit his head, from there moved to the hospital. They said he got tangled up, but it's clear from the video that he's being pushed. The guards entered, dominating.

LUST: Police reports must be verified.

GLUTTONY: Can you imagine if there were more videos of more abuse?

GOODNESS: Fortunately, people are protesting.

SLOTH: They should protest more.

LUST: Peacefully, which is the important thing.

GOODNESS: That's right.

GLUTTONY: In Buffalo they arrested two of the policemen, hundreds of them protested.

SLOTH: They entered dominating.

GLUTTONY: In Colombia, it was reported that the police beat Anderson Arboleda, a young black man, to death with a stick.

SLOTH: They applied the common phrase: "It will be investigated to the last consequences"

ALL THE DEATHS: Whoever falls (Pause) Wup! (Another tone) No one fell.

LUST: In Jalisco, Mexico, police officers murdered Giovanni López Medina, the protest did not let the case die.

GOODNESS: We must protest against abuse and racism.

ALL DEATHS: Without violence so as not to generate more of the same.

GOODNESS: We must protest against police brutality.

ALL DEATHS: Non-violent.

GOODNESS: We must protest against racism.

ALL DEATHS: Non-violent.

GOODNESS: The world protests.

GLUTTONY: In the main cities there is protest.

SLOTH: (Shows a sign that reads:) Black Lives Matter.

GOODNESS, GLUTTONY, AND LUST: (Applause and raise their voices of encouragement) Yeah!

PRIDE: On both sides there are good people.

WRATH: On both sides.

ENVY: On both sides.

GOODNESS: No to racism.

GLUTTONY: No to police abuse.

LUST: Without justice, there is no peace.

GOODNESS: Without justice, there is no peace.

LUST: Equality, equality.

GOODNESS: Love love, hate less.

(Gluttony has sat on a grave, from there he addresses Goodness)

GLUTTONY: Girl, come here.

(Goodness walks up to her)

GOODNESS: tell me

GLUTTONY: (advising) Don't pay much attention to Wrath and Pride, they always have a fight. (Another tone) You see this place, we are here because we belong here, but here there really is nothing else to look for.

GOODNESS: It is a holy place.

GLUTTONY: (What have you heard) Holy? This is full of bandits, corruption and sons of bitches.

GOODNESS: Also, there are good people here.

GLUTTONY: The bad ones are those of the noise.

GOODNESS: But there are good people.

SLOTH: There is everything here. Here, concave and convex meet.

LUST: Here, in this sacred place, (She covers her mouth as if correcting a mistake), sorry, I said (Another tone, as if remembering) ha yes, this here is full of everything. It's like a dunghill.

WRATH: And give your hatred to the world.

PRIDE: The stiff and motionless population here is made up of people from everywhere. There are rich and poor, believers and atheists. There are stupid and idiots who are the most and do not forget, there are of all races, of all creeds. There are dead people who seem dead, dead people who turned out beautiful, dead people who turned out ugly, dead people who seem alive (Pause) all dead and finished.

LUST: (Interrupting) And of all sexual preferences.

SLOTH: Those who the rest have forgotten.

GLUTTONY: (To Pride) How contemptuous you are.

PRIDE: Well, yes. This is a concoction that is only possible here.

GOODNESS: I think the grave bleachers have arrived.

ENVY: Because the money launderers are out there.

GREED: Here are some.

PRIDE: The poor things come, sweep and paint once a year as if that were enough.

GLUTTONY: It is more than enough, inside those boxes there is nothing left, worms, earthworms, bones and dust.

GREED: And some gold that could have gotten tangled up in a tooth.

SLOTH: Gluttony is right here, everyone arrives as they came into the world.

GLUTTONY: They were born with nothing, they came with nothing.

ALL DEATHS: The silver is still missing. (Pause {1, 2}) missing. It stays out there somewhere.

PRIDE: This one here (points to a grave) must have been important.

WRATH: Why do you think?

PRIDE: The tomb is like ceremonious.

WRATH: He was a pedophile priest. (Here everyone can take the bells and be ready to ring them later - Take them without ringing them)

GOODNESS: (Coming closer to the grave) Let's see... yes, pedophile and one of the worst.

PRIDE: Among them there are also good people.

LUST: Could there be? Everything is a mess. Plenty of morals from the mouth out.

SLOTH: They are abusers. Heavy hand, use a heavy hand against them.

ALL DEATHS: Heavy hand. (They ring some bells {1, 2, 3, 4, 5, 6}, they move, they stir) (Pause {1,2}) Hard hand (They ring the bells {1, 2, 3, 4, 5, 6 }) (Pause {1,2}) Firm hand (The bells ring {1, 2, 3, 4, 5, 6}).

LUST: The church has protected them for centuries.

GOODNESS: The church has also been dominant.

GLUTTONY: Dominant is the common denominator.

LUST: Some come at night.

GOODNESS: How?

LUST: Just as you hear it. Some of those pedophile priests come at night, when it's quiet and alone, to participate in some very strange covens. Gravediggers can attest. Some of those priests bring youngsters to whom they tell the story, many of the priests wear red shoes.

GOODNESS: I can't believe it

LUST: You better believe it.

GLUTTONY: I've seen them. As I saw the night burial of one who died of madness. Sick colleagues from the hospital where he was being treated accompanied him. That night there was a lot of messy dancing and a lot of marijuana.

GOODNESS: And nobody controlled them?

SLOTH: It is the freest and most dynamic burial celebrated in this holy field.

GLUTTONY: Field what?

SLOTH: Cemetery.

GLUTTONY: Now yes.

PRIDE: There is always fake news.

GLUTTONY: Here there are few fake news. Dead bodies to the grave.

GOODNESS: Do they tell everything?

SLOTH: Little matters to them in life, less after death.

GOODNESS: Who are the ones that count?

GLUTTONY: The mourners, the offended, the deceived, those who avenge their loved ones, those who slandered. Everyone, everyone counts. Those who have not yet committed suicide.

ENVY: You never miss an opportunity to smear.

SLOTH: They told about the princess who died making love to her dog.

GOODNESS: I can't believe it!

ENVY: Believe it.

GLUTTONY: Believe it.

GOODNESS: Doesn't it bother you so much lowliness?

ALL THE DEATHS: No, seeing and listening is our job

(Another tone) and death, of course.

GOODNESS: How do you do it?

ALL THE DEATHS: We like our work.

PRIDE: Here of sadness only one has been buried who was killed by lack of love.

ALL DEATHS: And we got it too.

GOODNESS: Wow!

ALL DEATHS: Died of an overdose of sadness.

GOODNESS: Wow!

ALL THE DEATHS: The deplorable thing you haven't mentioned.

GOODNESS: I don't even know what to think.

ALL DEATHS: Where do you leave the missing?

GOODNESS: I don't even want to think about it.

WRATH: This is an unavoidable ride.

GREED: The bad thing about getting here is leaving wealth out.

ENVY: You could try to bring it.

GREED: So you can have it?

ENVY: Who else?

GREED: It wouldn't be worth it.

ENVY: It was never worth it.

GLUTTONY: My short-term goal: eat, eat, eat.

SLOTH: Mine: sleep, rest and sleep.

GLUTTONY: Long term: eat, eat and eat.

SLOTH: Sleep more and rest more.

LUST: If the living would think of death, they would enjoy life more.

WRATH: It is impossible to think of death.

SLOTH: Some are arriving on the side of the one who died of poorly treated insomnia.

LUST: They should understand that everything, like pleasure, is temporary.

GREED: Wealth is not.

GLUTTONY: Sure it is.

PRIDE: The only certain and lasting thing is me.

ENVY: ha ha!

PRIDE: Nobody does it better than me, nobody knows more than me.

WRATH: We are fed up with your formula.

GLUTTONY: The memories will talk.

SLOTH: Of course they'll talk.

PRIDE: I'm fantastic.

ENVY: Me too.

PRIDE: I could tell you've done an impressive job.

WRATH: I would say the same about myself.

PRIDE: I'm not so sure.

WRATH: I am.

PRIDE: You are wrong.

GLUTTONY: (To Lust) It seems that your horniness has disappeared.

LUST: I took it off myself, (Flirty) as always.

GLUTTONY: Are you calmer?

LUST: I'm always calm but as a friend says: "when there's a party I'm here for the party"

GLUTTONY: To fuck corrupt politicians.

LUST: Always.

GREED: Nothing wrong with seeking your fortune.

GOODNESS: As long as it's honest.

WRATH: The politician should have special treatment.

SLOTH: Dedicate yourself to working for your country.

GREED: And save pesos.

ENVY: The peoples are in their debt.

GLUTTONY: It's what they believe.

PRIDE: The politician is the one who brings progress and work.

SLOTH: As long as he doesn't steal.

GREED: Stealing is human.

GOODNESS: And punishing too.

GLUTTONY: Some are pirates.

SLOTH: When one of those corrupt people arrives here, I don't look, I don't see, I don't care.

WRATH: The peoples owe them everything. They are patriots.

LUST: Most of them are good criminals.

GOODNESS: The law should be ruthless.

LUST: Many politicians should be as serious as the bandits.

GLUTTONY: A lot of ties and little honesty.

ENVY: They are cynical. And for me to say it... it is needed.

SLOTH: "Wonderful" said a thunder clap that fell in a meeting of bandit politicians.

GREED: Plutocracy, regardless of where the money comes from, is a proper way of life. It is the select group, the ideal group. They are the really good people.

PRIDE: To exercise progress, control and dominance.

SLOTH: I don't think so.

GLUTTONY: Don't tell me.

LUST: All that impresses me is the money I can get out of them for performing my favors. Some are so disgusting that, even with all the money they are not worth it.

SLOTH: There is one ahead that is embarrassing.

GOODNESS: How do you know?

SLOTH: We already told you that they tell everything.

SLOTH, GLUTTONY AND LUST: (Hands playing the sound of the musical key) Pla, pla, pla, Panama papers. Pla, pla, pla, Panama papers.

LUST: That one even stole toilet paper.

SLOTH: We don't like death, but it has its charms.

GLUTTONY: Here you see things that only the eyes believe.

LUST: We have seen funerals of bandits that are crowded and funerals of just men where the widow barely comes.

WRATH: In this place, life lived doesn't count and pomposity doesn't make sense, it never did.

ENVY: There will always be winners.

SLOTH: That's what you think.

ALL THE DEATHS: (There is a pause {1, 2}) (In chorus as they follow an imaginary character who passes between the tombstones and mausoleums-Some point at her). There goes Décima. With lots of wool and a new spinning wheel. Locking threads of life to allocate death (Pause {1, 2}-Reiterative as if they had already said it). The spindle is also new. (Pause {1,2}) Locking threads of life to allocate death.

WRATH: Hardly anyone remembers her.

LUST: She is not wrong, predicting destiny.

ENVY: People think they deserve it (Pause) if Décima doesn't offer it, there's nothing.

ALL DEATHS: There is nothing.

PRIDE: I am the owner of my own destiny.

ALL DEATHS: It is what you suppose.

PRIDE: (To Envy) Envy. Do you also believe that?

ENVY: Of course, but I model my part.

PRIDE: (To Sloth) Sloth, do you think so?

SLOTH: My destiny is clear, and I am happy with it. Sleep and rest, I do not want more.

PRIDE: (A Gluttony) You Gluttony, what do you say?

GLUTTONY: My thing is to eat, eat and nothing else.

PRIDE: (To Wrath) Wrath, dear friend. What do you say?

WRATH: I can't change anything, I'm arrogant.

PRIDE: (To Greed) Could you stop hoarding?

GREED: I want it all, and I'm not going to change.

PRIDE: Am I alone, then?

LUST: Didn't you know? Here each of us has a trade.

PRIDE: Occupation?

LUST: They call it sin, but it is a trade.

GOODNESS: Trades of evil.

LUST: No, it's a matter of free will.

GOODNESS: Animals don't have it.

LUST: They are better than many humans.

GOODNESS: It shouldn't even be said.

LUST: It's the truth.

GOODNESS: It all seems so confusing.

GLUTTONY: Confusing an oil spill in Russia.

SLOTH: Where?

GLUTTONY: Near Norilsk, in the Arctic.

ENVY: I don't believe it.

GLUTTONY: The Ambarnaya and Daldykan rivers are or were turned red from pollution.

SLOTH: And those responsible?

GLUTTONY: I'm fine, thank you.

GREED: They were producing.

SLOTH: Producing irresponsibly.

GREED: They'll clean up.

GLUTTONY: It will take more than 10 years.

GOODNESS: Unbelievable.

GLUTTONY: Instead of producing food they produce problems.

SLOTH: They only care about making currency bills.

GREED: That's called progress.

ENVY: Although some may not like it.

WRATH: Other people's progress produces anger.

GREED: It is searching for wealth for all.

GLUTTONY: For a few, I would say.

GREED: For those who deserve fortune, it's that easy.

ENVY: The rest let them wait in line.

WRATH: Their turn will come.

SLOTH: My turn has come.

LUST: Bad at sex, terrible, they never have time.

GLUTTONY: They are destroying everything.

GOODNESS: With the planet and with the animals.

LUST: And some say no.

GOODNESS: Nonsense seems to be right.

LUST: Like slander and fake news.

SLOTH: Can you imagine this before social networks?

GLUTTONY: Entire generations deceived.

PRIDE: Believing and defending lying concepts.

LUST: We are part of that example.

GOODNESS: Half of what I learned is a lie.

GLUTTONY: More, I would say.

SLOTH: Simple: the powerful lie and instill fear.

GLUTTONY: People don't question out of fear.

GOODNESS: Now with the socoial networks, at least there is questioning.

LUST: People are irreverent, that's important.

PRIDE: There is a lot of fake news.

GOODNESS: Among the false ones there are true ones, before they were all manipulated.

SLOTH: Some warned of the falsehoods, but they were erased from the map.

GLUTTONY: They blot them out.

PRIDE: They prevented the normal development of business.

ENVY: They complained of envy.

WRATH: Governments used little force.

GLUTTONY: Wow!

WRATH: Domination Against Insurrection.

SLOTH: And freedom?

PRIDE: Freedom must belong to the rulers to maintain healthy governments.

SLOTH: Healthy for whom?

WRATH: For the rulers, of course.

PRIDE: They watch over the welfare of the people.

GOODNESS: (walks over to the coffin) Speaking of lies.

WRATH: Pinocchio?

GLUTTONY: Do you hear the noise of the pots?

SLOTH: No noise, please.

GLUTTONY: They're coming to the funeral of this poor thing who died of anorexia.

GOODNESS: Many people die from it.

GLUTTONY: She wanted to look good, and she was only bones. I do not share the idea.

GOODNESS: Poor thing.

ENVY: The competition is strong.

WRATH: I wanted to be more beautiful than the rest.

SLOTH: It didn't work.

LUST: It never works. Those of us who are beautiful, are beautiful.

PRIDE: The concepts and ideas belong to each one.

SLOTH: Not the deceitful ones.

GOODNESS: Some deaths should be undone.

ALL DEATHS: Not that!

WRATH: If they are fooled, it is their problem.

GLUTTONY: They ask them to look pretty without realizing that beauty is fleeting.

PRIDE: (To Gluttony) Yours was, it didn't last long.

GLUTTONY: I feel good.

ENVY: Nobody envies you, and that's sad.

GLUTTONY: Sad for you.

SLOTH: It is part of the lying teachings.

PRIDE: I love myself, I know I love myself.

(Lust has disappeared. The sound of a vibrator is heard in the distance)

WRATH: Again?

LUST: (Affirmative) Again.

GLUTTONY: She and her body.

SLOTH: She and her body.

ENVY: She should be more populist.

GREED: She couldn't live from the poor.

GLUTTONY: Everyone likes sex.

GREED: Not the expensive kind.

SLOTH: Sex is sex.

GREED: No, no. The expensive one is more lascivious.

GOODNESS: Less sincere.

GREED: More enjoyable.

GOODNESS: The poor enjoy love.

GREED: They have not discovered the interested party.

GOODNESS: Please!

GREED: The business of sex is more accommodating.

GOODNESS: It's fake.

WRATH: Life is largely faked.

ENVY: Few live a real life.

PRIDE: Most like to show off.

WRATH: They want to be important.

PRIDE: They pretend to be what they are not.

ENVY: They read the horoscope.

SLOTH: Most people are fascinated by it.

GLUTTONY: It tells them what they are not and what they like.

ENVY: A little motivation doesn't hurt.

SLOTH: But they believe the story.

PRIDE: That's how they are, that's why a few of us dominate.

GOODNESS: It should be different.

SLOTH: The horoscope calms the nerves of many.

ENVY: And Facebook too. They see themselves or try to see themselves in a mirror that is seen nearby, but is distant and unattainable.

GLUTTONY: It justifies many others.

GOODNESS: None of that is true.

PRIDE: They believe it and that is
.

WRATH: Enough to keep them asleep.

ENVY: Show them another movie.

SLOTH: They won't see it because that means they could lose.

WRATH: Nobody likes to lose.

GLUTTONY: You have to be realistic.

PRIDE: For what?

SLOTH: To face life in another way.

PRIDE: That wouldn't solve anything for them.

WRATH: It is better that they believe the story.

ENVY: That way they will be calm
.

LUST: (gives a satisfied exclamation)

GOODNESS: (walks over to the coffin) We have a problem here.

GREED: A no name?

GOODNESS: (Pulls a mask out of the coffin and shows it)

ALL DEATHS: Coronavirus!

PRIDE: Those are not supposed to be buried, they are cremated.

ENVY: Be careful. From Wuhan, it's very contagious.

WRATH: And is there another one?

ENVY: For now only the Wuhan one, with its variants, more than enough.

GREED: A plague.

ENVY: A new one, many more to come.

GLUTTONY: Little is known about the coronavirus.

SLOTH: It is deadly for certain people.

GOODNESS: Conjectures and comments but little more concrete.

GREED: It took us by surprise.

GOODNESS: There were warnings from responsible people, but no one listened.

SLOTH: How did it appear?

GOODNESS: At a wet market in Wuhan, China.

GLUTTONY: Wet?

GOODNESS: They call them that because the floor is always wet.

GLUTTONY: Wet?

GOODNESS: They kill and clean dead animals, waste falls on the floor and that is why they keep it wet.

PRIDE: It was created in a laboratory.

GOODNESS: It's guesswork. Not proven, just conjectures. News, you all know.

WRATH: Those Chinese.

GOODNESS: There are many viruses, many coronaviruses, there is no need to create them.

ENVY: This one is strong.

GLUTTONY: It's a plague.

SLOTH: Spreads easily.

GOODNESS: The news is grim.

GLUTTONY: Enough to be terrified.

WRATH: People beg for help in hospitals.

GOODNESS: There is no cure.

GREED: We have to find one.

LUST: They should have thought about it longer.

WRATH: Health systems can't cope.

SLOTH: People are dying like flies.

GLUTTONY: We were not prepared.

PRIDE: We have always been prepared.

GLUTTONY: You're wrong, we didn't even know how to wash our hands.

GOODNESS: They say that old people are left to die.

PRIDE: Between saving an old man, and saving a young man there is not much to think about.

WRATH: The old must make room for the young.

GREED: Old people don't work, old people cost money.

GOODNESS: What you say is a sin.

WRATH: Old people die alone.

GREED: The economy is more important than everything.

ENVY: The old ones have already paid their dues.

SLOTH: You all are a disgrace.

PRIDE: The destiny of retired old people is death. What else are you worried about?

GREED: They cost too much.

WRATH: The children could take care of the parents.

GLUTTONY: Most don't have the resources.

WRATH: The elderly are just memories, medicines and social burden.

SLOTH: The old ones built all of this.

WRATH: They built, past tense like you said.

GLUTTONY: People are afraid.

PRIDE: Because they want to be. This is a flu, a flu.

ENVY: They should let all the old ones die, it would cost less and revitalize the economy.

WRATH: So said Dan Patrick, Lieutenant Governor of Texas.

GLUTTONY: How old is he?

SLOTH: More than 70.

GLUTTONY: Did he commit suicide?

GOODNESS: No.

GLUTTONY: He should have set the example.

GOODNESS: Many are pure blah blah.

SLOTH: Do you remember "Buche y Plumas no más".

GOODNESS: Rafael Hernandez.

SLOTH: That's how most of them are.

LUST: Do as I say, not as I do.

GLUTTONY: What the fuck!

GREED: They don't understand economics.

GOODNESS: Not the rich ones.

ENVY: They don't understand anything.

GLUTTONY: People are afraid.

PRIDE: Everything will be under control.

WRATH: We have to get people out of quarantine.

GOODNESS: Isolate to avoid infections.

GREED: Meanwhile, the economy is dying.

GOODNESS: No economy is worth more than people.

ENVY: If they don't work, they will starve.

PRIDE: Let them try chloroquine or injections of liquid soap.

LUST: Let the governments put their hands in their pockets.

GREED: A solution would cost a lot.

GOODNESS: Governments have bailed out private enterprise many times.

GREED: The companies are the ones that provide work.

GLUTTONY: People don't want to go out.

SLOTH: They are afraid.

GLUTTONY: They fear for the elderly.

ENVY: We already talked about the elderly.

GLUTTONY: They fear for them.

GREED: The State is the most important thing.

GOODNESS: The States proved that they are bankrupt.

ENVY: Don't talk nonsense.

GOODNESS: The pandemic brought the truth out.

GREED: Which truth?

GOODNESS: All those riches were not solid. The world panicked, economies were decimated. It seems that everything was pure bluff.

WRATH: Thats if there is no production.

SLOTH: Where is the wealth?

GLUTTONY: With a single shake, everything seems to end.

GOODNESS: This has shown the true colors.

GLUTTONY: A lot of blah blah and little truth.

SLOTH: Pandemic announcement and the world collapses.

PRIDE: It's the fault of the Chinese.

WRATH: We have to be strong.

GOODNESS: The number of unemployed is in the millions.

GLUTTONY: The dead ones too.

SLOTH: Vaccines appeared.

WRATH: That's right.

ENVY: They will return to the new normal.

GLUTTONY: It's like a new diet. It doesn't work.

PRIDE: The coronavirus will disappear as it came.

ENVY: It's not very clear.

WRATH: People must work.

GOODNESS: Inequality is accentuated. Poverty increases.

WRATH: Precisely, they have to work.

GLUTTONY: They are afraid of getting infected.

PRIDE: They will die from the virus or from hunger if they don't work.

GOODNESS: The States ought to put their hands in their pockets.

ENVY: It is a very high cost and only rich countries can face the pandemic.

SLOTH: They could take a little away from the war budget.

PRIDE: We would weaken.

GLUTTONY: We are well-prepared to face war. But we run faced with a pandemic.

GOODNESS: Can you imagine if it had been an atomic bomb?

SLOTH: Not even thinking about it. The coronavirus collapsed health systems.

GLUTTONY: No one is ready.

SLOTH: Nobody.

GOODNESS: Prepared to attack: yes. What if they attack us?

PRIDE: We are ready.

GLUTTONY: Don't think so. We didn't even know how to wash our hands.

LUST: The mere announcement of the virus turned the world upside down.

WRATH: We need to produce.

GOODNESS: We need to eradicate Covid.

PRIDE: We work fast.

GLUTTONY: But with each vaccine, a new variant.

WRATH: Meanwhile, we have to work.

LUST: People are afraid of contagion.

ENVY: They are more afraid of hunger.

GOODNESS: You have to find a lasting way out.

PRIDE: Go to the new normal.

LUST: Were we ever normal?

GOODNESS: Well, look around.

GLUTTONY: Find a way out.

SLOTH: Otherwise everything will collapse, there will be hunger, crime, horror.

GOODNESS: Not to mention mental problems.

SLOTH: The suicides started, and the divorces don't seem to stop.

PRIDE: There have always been crazy people, there have always been suicides, there have always been divorces.

SLOTH: Divorces increase exponentially.

GLUTTONY: This quarantine takes people out of time and place.

GOODNESS: Some know how to handle it.

GLUTTONY: Who?

GOODNESS: Artists are always creating in isolation.

PRIDE: Those are the artists.

GREED: They can't sell.

GLUTTONY: They can produce.

GREED: The most important thing is to sell.

GLUTTONY: For most of them: produce.

WRATH: The stage artists are fried.

GREED: They've canceled everything.

PRIDE: They have closed the stadiums.

WRATH: They will open, the politicians are working on it.

LUST: Webcam dolls make a fortune.

PRIDE: They are happy.

GREED: Excellent merchants.

WRATH: Soon there will be a permanent opening, politicians are working on it.

GLUTTONY: Politicians are not scientists.

GOODNESS: This is a matter of a joint effort.

PRIDE: You sound like a politician.

ENVY: Small merchants are throwing in the towel.

GOODNESS: Many have thrown everything away.

GREED: Including debts.

WRATH: They are irresponsible.

GOODNESS: Some can't take it anymore.

ENVY: You defend the indefensible.

WRATH: Why don't you kill yourself with them?

GOODNESS: Inequality is not cured with deaths, solutions are needed.

GLUTTONY: Job opportunities.

PRIDE: Why we should open, open and open definitively, not that opening one day and closing the next.

SLOTH: If this pandemic has taught us anything, it is that no matter how big the capital is, if it is left alone, it is useless.

PRIDE: Companies and businesses must be opened, the cost has already be paid. On the way, the masses are satisfied.

GLUTTONY: Many are afraid.

ENVY: Then let them starve.

WRATH: Let them starve.

GOODNESS: It wouldn't be fair.

GREED: You have been told that justice does not exist.

GLUTTONY: You have to find a way.

SLOTH: Let them come out, let them lose their fear.

GOODNESS: There is no other way out. We need a 100% guaranteed cure or vaccine.

PRIDE: Work.

ENVY: Yes, work.

GREED: Fight the unemployment that is ruining us.

WRATH: Work and nothing else.

GOODNESS: And health?

PRIDE: Some will die, as in everything, but the economy will be saved. In wars, heroes have set the example.

GREED: We will be big, rich and powerful, that's what counts.

WRATH: The poor and the old who are vacating.

LUST: It is an infamy.

PRIDE: It is life.

GLUTTONY: Life is eating.

SLOTH: Life is sleep.

GOODNESS: Life is being better with others.

PRIDE: That doesn't make any sense. Everyone manages as its possible.

ENVY: If you are good, they will envy you.

WRATH: They will make fun of you.

GOODNESS: If there is no justice, crime will increase.

PRIDE: Impossible, we will dominate. Implement Law and Order.

GOODNESS: Hunger is stronger than honesty.

GLUTTONY: If there are more outbreaks, panic will take over everything.

SLOTH: It would be worse.

PRIDE: With time it will disappear.

GOODNESS: Sit back and wait for the last summer.

GLUTTONY: Many are returning to the fields.

PRIDE: Food is needed.

GLUTTONY: Many really.

WRATH: This virus has fucked up life.

GOODNESS: It showed that we are all equal.

GREED: Equal?

GOODNESS: Yes, equals, it attacks everyone equally. It doesn't knock on the door, it comes in.

GLUTTONY: Fear spread all over.

SLOTH: In the one that crosses, you don't see an enemy, you see a contagion.

GOODNESS: People are afraid.

PRIDE: Honestly, there aren't even that many dead.

GLUTTONY: There are many.

SLOTH: There is sadness, those who sang no longer sing and those who cried have no tears left.

GOODNESS: Learning to live with the virus, it is what it is.

GLUTTONY: Nobody knows about coronavirus.

GOODNESS: We need truths, vaccines and lasting cures.

PRIDE: It is important that a friend find it.

GREED: It would be a stroke of genius and fortune.

WRATH: For now there is no absolute protection.

GOODNESS, GLUTTONY, SLOTH AND LUST: Cure or Vaccine guaranteed.

PRIDE AND GREED: Let a friend find her.

GOODNESS, GLUTTONY, SLOTH AND LUST: Cure or Vaccine guaranteed.

PRIDE AND GREED: It would be a stroke of genius and fortune.

GOODNESS, GLUTTONY, SLOTH AND LUST: Cure or vaccine, heritage of all.

PRIDE, GREED, ANGER AND ENVY: Always putting buts.

PRIDE AND GREED: Let a friend find her. It would be a stroke of genius and fortune.

ALL THE DEATHS: (Pause {1, 2}) (In chorus as they follow an imaginary character who passes between the tombstones and mausoleums-Some point at her). There goes Morta. With lots of wool and a new spinning wheel. Cutting threads of life to dictate death (Pause {1, 2} - Repetitive as if they had already said it). The spindle is also new (Pause {1, 2}) Cutting threads of life to dictate death.

LUST: Oh no. Morta stood behind Goodness.

GLUTTONY AND SLOTH: It can't be, it shouldn't be.

PRIDE: Sure, it is.

WRATH AND ENVY: Goodness is a stone in the shoe.

PRIDE, WRATH AND ENVY: No death can be annulled.

ALL DEATHS EXCEPT LUST: None, it is our job.

PRIDE: Goodness must not die.

PRIDE, WRATH AND ENVY: Goodness is a stone in the shoe.

(The deaths, minus Lust, surround Goodness who after a struggle fades and falls dead)

LUST: (loudly) It's not the death of me! Mind you, it's not my death! She was good, that's why you finished her. I am only joy, that's why you hate me. It is not my death. Neither she should have died, nor am I a sin.

THE DEATHS MINUS THE LUST: It is our job (They are getting closer to Lust) It is our job, we are death. (Lust escapes) (The deaths whispering) We are death, it is our job, we are death. (They go to the place where the piece began) (In a more audible voice) We are death, it is our job, We are death, it is our job.. (The light and the sound of the voices of the deaths that have been repeated are lowered. (Pause {1, 2} The sound of a vibrator is heard. Darkness)

END

The rehersals

From left to right: Sasha I Rivera, Amparo Cordero, Ana María Hamilton, Hilda González, Geraldine Campo, Joan Amaya, Katiria De La Cruz and Ana Milena Campo.

Ana Milena Campo

From left to right, Katiria De La Cruz, Joan Amaya, Ana María Hamilton, Amparo Cordero, Geraldine Campo and Sasha I Rivera who had her birthday celebrated.

Ana María Hamilton

From left to right: Joan Amaya, Amparo Cordero, Ana María Hamilton, Hilda González, Katiria De La Cruz, Geraldine Campo and Ana Milena Campo.

Katiria De La Cruz

Sasha I Rivera (left) y Joan Amaya.

Geraldine Campo

Geraldine Campo (left) y Katiria De La Cruz.

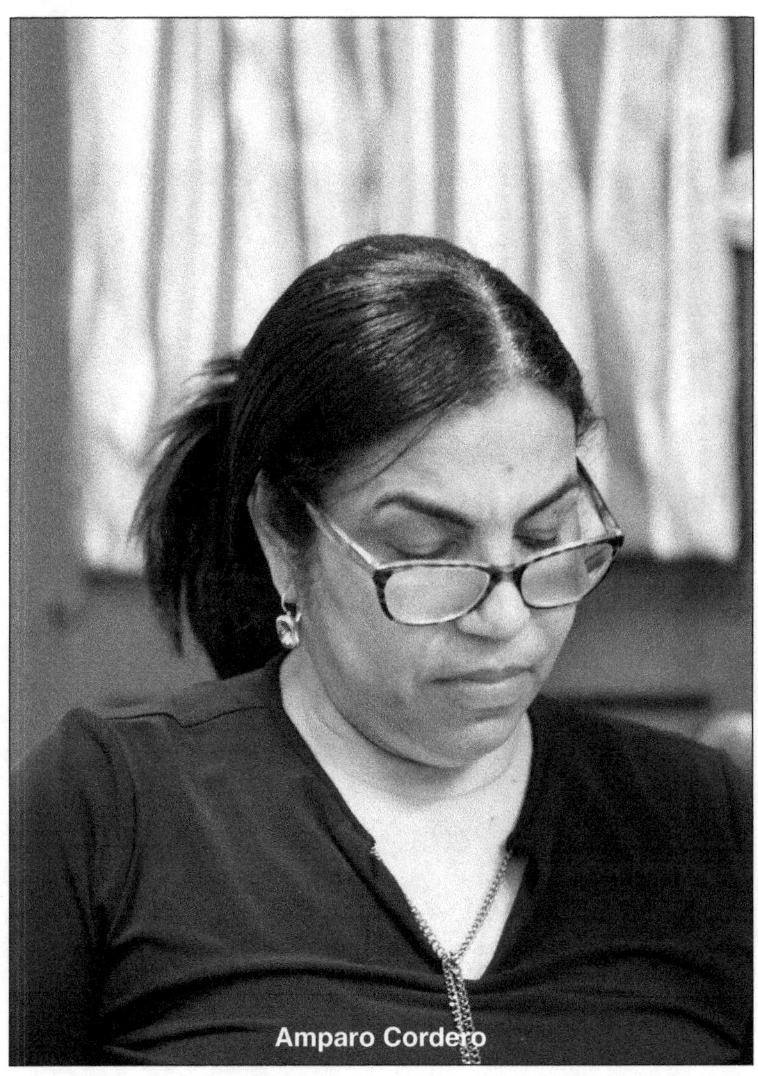
Amparo Cordero

From left to right. Back: Sasha I Rivera and Hilda González, in front: Geraldine Campo and Amparo Cordero.

Sasha I Rivera

From left to right: Ana María Hamilton, Hilda González and Geraldine Campo.

Hilda González

Left to right: Geraldine Campo, Ana Milena Campo and José Díaz.

Joan Amaya

From left to right: Amparo Cordero, Katiria De La Cruz, Ana María Hamilton, Geraldine Campo, Ana Milena Campo, and Sasha I Rivera showing one of the announcements for the May 14, 2022 reading.

First reading
May 14, 2022
1425 W Linden St
Allentown, PA 18102

Sábado 14 de mayo de 2022 - 7 PM

presenta:

Entre lápidas y mausoleos

Obra de teatro escrita y dirigida por José Díaz

La primera lectura (estreno) se realizará el sábado 14 de mayo de 2022 a las 7 de la noche en Allentown, PA - Todos están invitados pero por razones de espacio y distanciamiento social, es necesario hacer una reservación llamando al 570.657.6812

Con:

Amparo Cordero - Ana María Hamilton
Ana Milena Campo - Geraldine Campo
Hilda González - Joan Amaya
Katiria De La Cruz - Sasha I Rivera

"Entre lápidas y mausoleos", escrita por José Díaz, es un interesante encuentro que ocurre entre los siete pecados capitales personificados por catrinas y la Bondad, en medio de lápidas y mausoleos en un cementerio cualquiera.
Los diálogos, sin tapujos, son reveladores e irreverentes. El espectador encontrará, muy seguramente, una forma distinta de ver la realidad en que vivimos.

Solo para mayores de 18 años

The first reading was held on Saturday, May 14, 2022 at 7 p.m. at 1425 West Linden Street in Allentown, Pennsylvania, United States, with the following cast in order of appearance:

Lust - Ana Milena Campo
Envy - Ana Maria Hamilton
Pride - Katiria De La Cruz
Wrath - Geraldine Campo
Goodness - Amparo Cordero
Sloth - Sasha I Rivera
Gluttony- Hilda Gonzalez
Greed - Joan Amaya

Writer and director - José Díaz

This reading was filmed and can be seen on the YouTube channel: Jose Díaz-Escritor

Ana Milena Campo.......... Lust

40 years old, born in Barranquilla, Colombia. Professional masseuse, single, mother of 3 children. Ana Milena considers herself charismatic, sociable and fun. She likes to read and dance. She loves sunsets and the sea.

Ana Milena Campo

Ana María Hamilton.......... Envy

She was born in Holguin, Cuba. She studied Fine Arts, painting and plastic arts in Cuba, Spain and the United States. She dedicated to painting. Her works have been exhibited in Allentown, Philadelphia, New York, Miami, Los Angeles, Barcelona and Cuba. She loves her family, friends, art and freedom.

Ana María Hamilton

Katiria De La Cruz.......... Pride

Dominicana, casada y madre de dos niños. Activista dedicada a colaborar en las organizaciones que apoyan, motivan y organizan a los latinoamericanos en Allentown, Hazleton y en Penn State University.

Katiria De La Cruz

Geraldine Campo.......... Wrath

She was born in Caracas, Venezuela. She is a graphic designer by profession. Furthermore, she enjoys traveling and outdoor activities.

Geraldine Campo

Amparo Cordero.......... Goodness

Born in Nagua, Dominican Republic. She graduated in education and family therapy. She is married with three children. She loves nature and life. Not only that, but she is committed to educational, cultural and community projects.

Amparo De La Cruz

Sasha I Rivera.......... Sloth

She was born in Puerto Rico, a single mother of 2 children. She defines herself as an entrepreneur and self-confident. Sasha affirms that on her back she carries a backpack full of optimism.

Sasha I Rivera

Hilda González.......... Gluttony

She was born in Monterrey, Mexico. She graduated in Communication Sciences. She is the founder of ICDI (Mexican Cultural Interlace and Integral Development). She founded the dance group "Sin Fronteras". Furthermore, she hosts the talk show "Tendencia VIP". She loves her family.

Hilda González

Joan Amaya.......... Greed

A native of Newark, NJ., of a Peruvian father and a Puerto Rican mother. Since 2008 she has done work in commercials, comedy, theater, music videos and feature films in English. This is her first work in Spanish.

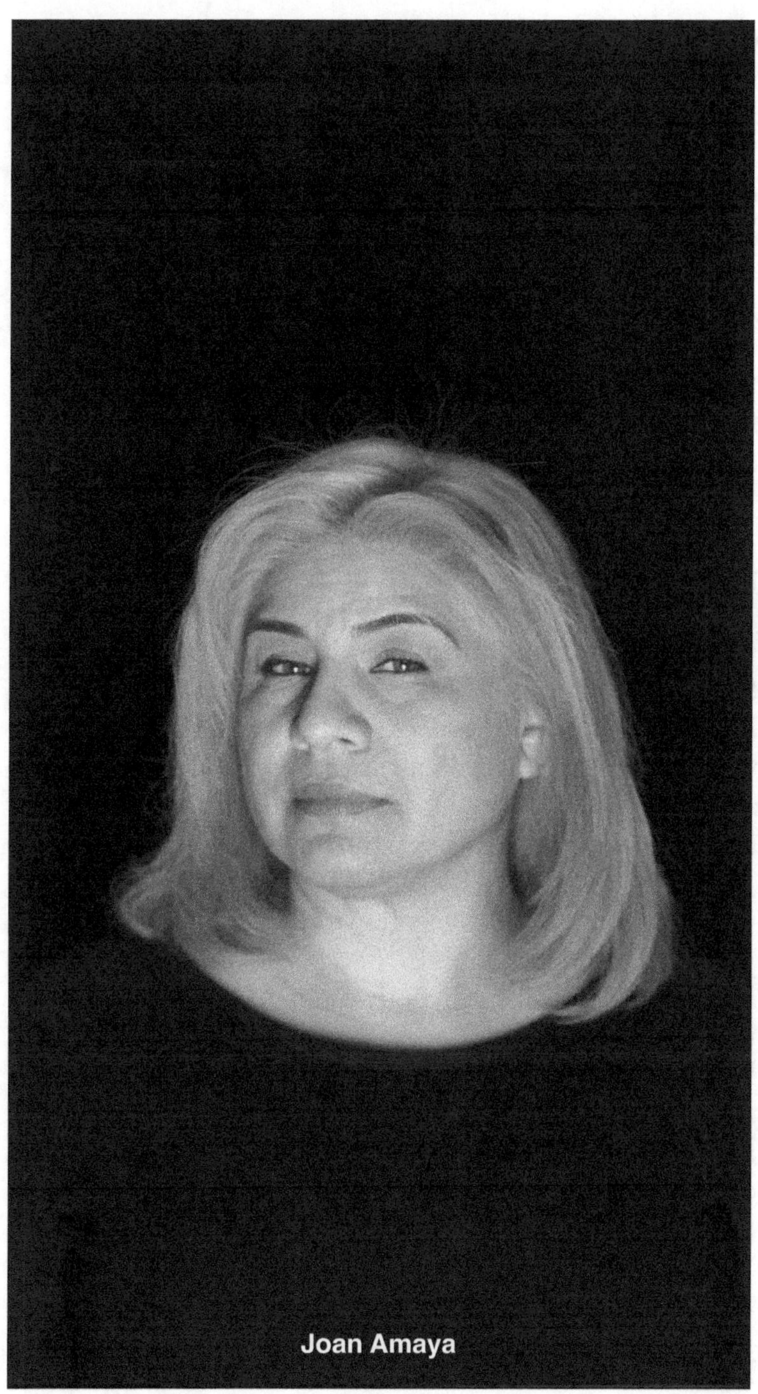

Joan Amaya

José Díaz, José Díaz, Born in Cali, Colombia (1953), he finished his degree in Management and Marketing and an MBA in Management at the World University in Puerto Rico. At Lehigh County Community College in Pennsylvania, she earned an associate's degree in accounting. At New York University, she graduated in international business. In 1977, he married Danilza Velázquez.

In 2002, he founded and is editor of the newspaper "Panorama Latin News", which circulates every other Wednesdays in Philadelphia and neighboring cities in the United States.

In 2012 José Díaz published: "I candidate: I propose, I promise, I commit myself." A book with interviews with 9 Dominican presidential candidates and "The Book of Epitaphs" (fiction). In 2013 he published: "Pupi" Legarreta, Salsa is named after him". An authorized biography of Félix "Pupi" Legarreta. In 2020 he wrote the play "Between tombstones and mausoleums". In 2021 the authorized biography of the Dominican musician Cuco Valoy (Award Winning Author, International Latino Book Awards 2022) and the book "RETRATOS / PORTRAITS" in which he presents a selection of photos taken during 40 years of journalistic practice and photography enthusiast. He began 2022 with a revised edition of "Between Tombstones and Mausoleums", the piece whose first reading was held on May 14, 2022 at 1425 West Linden Street in Allentown in the State of Pennsylvania in the United States. He has written and directed several short films that can be seen on the Mowies platform and on YouTube on the page: "José Díaz. Escritor". In 2017: ¿HOW HAS YOUR DAY BEEN?" and SELFI in 2018.

José is a ceramicist that makes sculptures in wood and steel.

José Díaz

From left to right. Back row: Joan Amaya, Katiria De La Cruz, Ana María Hamilton, Sasha I Rivera. In the front row: Hilda González, Amparo Cordero, José Díaz, Geraldine Campo and Ana Milena Campo.

The public
May 14, 2022
1425 W Linden St
Allentown, PA 18102

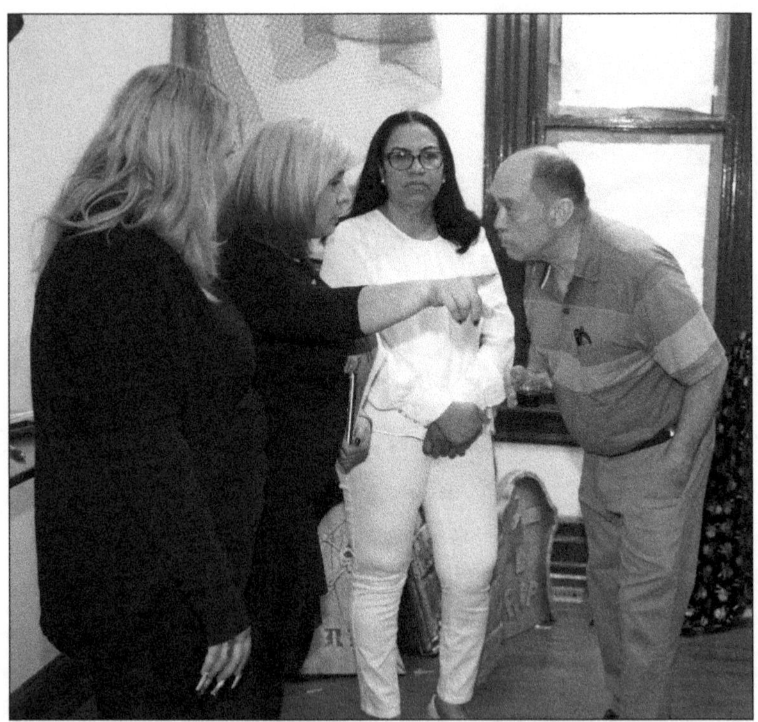

From left to right: Sasha I Rivera, Joan Amaya, Amparo Cordero and Bruce Fritzinger.

From left to right: Danilza Velázquez, Michael Lebson, Kate Hughes and Ana María Hamilton.

Alan Levin

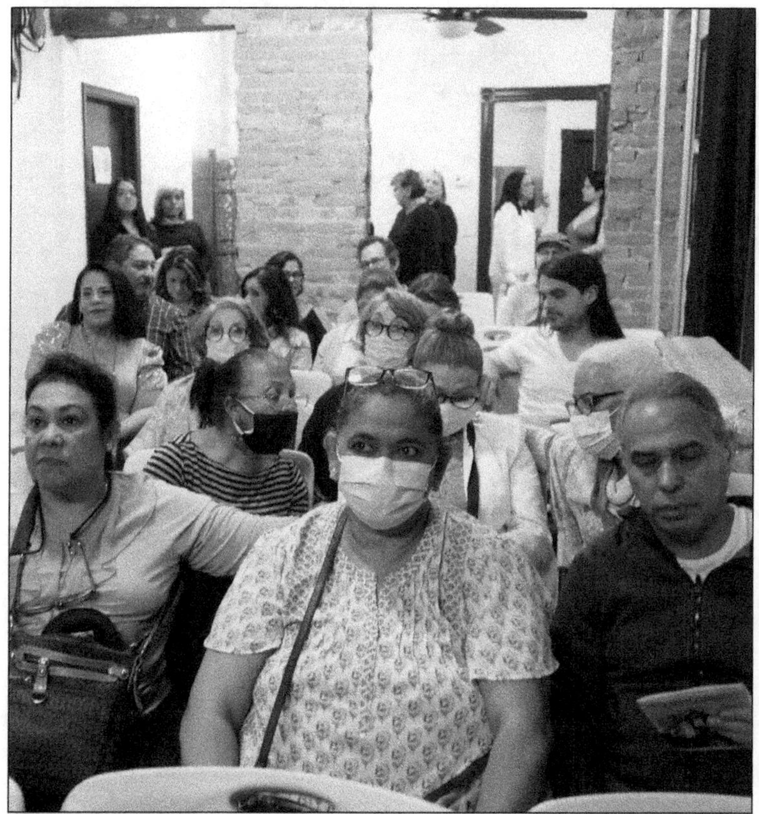

Part of the public that attended the first reading on May 14, 2022 in Allentown, PA.

José Taveras

Part of the public that attended the first reading on May 14, 2022 in Allentown, PA.

Noelia Ortiz-Lightner (left) and Joan Amaya.

From left to right: Kurt Woods, José Díaz, Christopher Shorr and Alberto Espinoza.

A group of friends shares once the reading is finished.

De izquierda a derecha: Rosmary Ortíz Soto , Olga Negrón, Marigny Pellot y Alani Jiménez.

Three friends share impressions about "Between tombstones and mausoleums" after reading.

Touchstone Theatre
July 30, 2022
321 E 4th Street
Bethlehem, PA 18015

TOUCHSTONE
THEATRE
Theatre that Transforms

Sábado 30 de julio de 2022 - 8 PM

en asociación con Touchstone Theatre's Latinx Initiative y Panorama CULTURAL

321 E 4th St, Bethlehem, PA 18015

presentan la lectura de la obra:

Entre lápidas y mausoleos

Obra de teatro escrita y dirigida por José Díaz

Con:

Amparo Cordero - Ana María Hamilton
Ana Milena Campo - Mildred Canelo
Hilda González - Joan Amaya
Katiria De La Cruz - Sasha I Rivera

"Entre lápidas y mausoleos", escrita por José Díaz, es un interesante encuentro que ocurre entre los siete pecados capitales personificados por catrinas y la Bondad, en medio de lápidas y mausoleos en un cementerio cualquiera.
Los diálogos, sin tapujos, son reveladores e irreverentes. El espectador encontrará, muy seguramente, una forma distinta de ver la realidad en que vivimos.
La presentación es en español pero se ofrecerá una sipnosis en inglés.

CONTENT WARNING: This play contains adult themes and strong language, and is not suitable for children.
Esta pieza teatral contiene lenguage y temas para adultos y solo se admiten personas mayores de 18 años.

La entrada es gratuita - Más información 570.657.6812

On Saturday, July 30, 2022, at 4 p.m. a reading was performed at the Touchstone Theatre, 321 E 4th Street, Bethlehem, Pennsylvania, United States, with the following cast in order of appearance:

Lust - Ana Milena Campo
Envy - Ana Maria Hamilton
Pride - Katiria De La Cruz
Wrath - Mildred Canelo
Goodness - Amparo Cordero
Sloth - Sasha I Rivera
Gluttony- Hilda Gonzalez
Greed - Joan Amaya

Writer and director - José Díaz

This reading was filmed and can be seen on the YouTube channel: Jose Díaz-Escritor

Ana Milena Campo

Ana María Hamilton

Katiria De La Cruz

Mildred Canelo

Amparo Cordero

Sasha I Rivera

Hilda González

Joan Amaya

José Díaz

José Díaz is an Award Winning Author of International Latino Book Awards.

www.ingramcontent.com/pod-product-compliance
Lightning Source LLC
LaVergne TN
LVHW010608160826
845677LV00013B/3314

* 9 7 9 8 3 7 0 5 6 9 6 6 1 *